The Green Men of Gressingham

by

Philip Ardagh

Illustrated by Mike Phillips

You do not need to read this page - just get on with the book!

First published 2002 in Great Britain by
Barrington Stoke Ltd
10 Belford Terrace, Edinburgh, EH4 3DQ

Copyright © 2002, Philip Ardagh
Illustrations © Mike Phillips
The moral right of the author has been asserted in accordance with
the Copyright, Designs and Patents Act 1988
ISBN 1-84299-085-3

Printed by Polestar AUP Aberdeen Ltd

MEET THE AUTHOR - PHILIP ARDAGH

What is your favourite animal?
A galliwasp
What is your favourite boy's name?
"Oi, you!"
What is your favourite girl's name?
Heloise (because that's the name of the girl who
grew up to marry me
What is your favourite food?
A large portion (I'm greedy!)
What is your favourite music?
It depends what mood I'm in -
sad music makes me happy
What is your favourite hobby?
Collecting old books (not ones
I've written myself!)

MEET THE ILLUSTRATOR - MIKE PHILLIPS

What is your favourite animal?
Dog
What is your favourite boy's name?
Ben (my son's name)
What is your favourite girl's name?
Hannah and Olivia
(my daughters)
What is your favourite food?
Cheese
What is your favourite music?
Anything that makes my
feet tap
What is your favourite hobby?
Armchair cricket supporting

For
Green Man
and
the rest of the 'A' Team

Contents

Robyn-in-the-Hat

Fidget

Friendly

Big Jim

Tom

Introduction

Meet the Green Men of Gressingham, a medieval band of robbers and outlaws dressed in brown. *Brown?* Well, yes. It's cheaper than green and it hides the dirt better.

This band is led by their masked mistress, Robyn-in-the-Hat. There's Big Jim, Friendly, Fidget and many more and they're about to take someone prisoner – Tom Dashwood, the hero of this tale!

Chapter 1
Up Before the Cock Crows

Tom Dashwood was up before the cock crowed, which wasn't as early as you might think because it was a Friday. Though the cock started crowing at dawn most days, it had a little lie-in on Fridays.

It was still pretty early however, and the servants had only been up five hours when Tom came into the great hall.

The straw the servants used for their bedding had been cleared away ages ago, and Cook had laid some breakfast on the long table.

Tom and his family didn't usually have breakfast together but this was not a normal Friday.

The day before, a big man had arrived at the Manor House. He wore a floppy hat shaped like a round, squishy loaf of bread. His name was Able Morris and he had been sent by Tom's uncle, Lord Dashwood, to take Tom back to Dashwood Castle so that the boy could train to be a page.

All those hundreds of years ago, training to be a page and then a squire, were the first steps towards becoming a real, live knight!

Tom had been so excited he had hardly slept. Ever since he could remember, he'd been looking forward to going to Dashwood Castle to train to be one of his uncle's knights. And now, at last, that day had come.

He'd spent much of the night seeing himself in sword fights and mock battles. The sound of horses' hooves and the cheering of the crowds had thundered in his ears.

It was Tom's mother, Lady Ann, who thought that a farewell breakfast would be a nice idea. It was her one last chance to spend a little time with her son before he left. She was very pleased for him but, at the same time, she was sad to see him go. Most mums are like that.

Because it was so early in the day, everyone drank 'small' beer and not the strong stuff. *Small* beer? Well, like all men and women of noble birth, they never drank water from their well because it was usually a horrid brown colour and tasted like mud. So they always drank beer and small beer was the weakest.

Now the day had arrived, his mother wasn't hungry, so she chewed her hanky instead. Her eyes were red and swollen and she looked as though she'd been lying awake all night. That was because she had been. She'd been thinking of her little boy leaving home.

"I propose a toast," said Tom's father, Sir Simon, rising to his feet. "To my son, Thomas, on his first step on the road to honour and glory!"

"Honour and glory," agreed Able Morris, and everyone raised their goblets to their lips. Tom felt so proud that his face glowed bright red.

"We must take our leave of you now, Sir Simon," said Able Morris. "Tom and I have a long ride and a dusty road ahead of us."

Everyone, even the servants, went to the front of the Manor House to see Tom on his way.

Lady Ann's hanky wasn't only wet from the chewing now, but also from her tears. "Be brave and true, Tom," she said.

Tom's father gave him a hug. Then Able Morris leant forward on his huge horse, grabbed Tom by the hand and yanked him up onto the animal's back.

Tom sat behind Able Morris and secretly hoped that he wouldn't ride too fast. There was no way that he could put his arms around the man's waist to hold on. It was far too wide.

Able Morris turned his head – squishy hat and all. He looked at Tom. "It's time we we were off, Master Tom!"

With 'goodbyes' and 'good lucks' ringing in their ears, Tom, Able Morris and Able's horse, Ferdy, set off to ride to the castle.

Chapter 2
Gressingham Forest

To begin with, they passed through places Tom knew well. These were places he'd been to with his father – the village, the church, the field where the Harvest Fair was held each year.

Soon they were travelling through countryside Tom had only ever seen from far off.

Tom turned in the saddle and could no longer see the Manor House, though he could still make out the very top of the church tower, poking above the trees.

"We'll be coming to Gressingham Forest soon, Master Tom," said Able. "There be outlaws in that place, so say not a word and hold on tight, for we may have to make a quick escape."

Tom felt both fear and excitement. They'd been gone less than a day and already he was in the middle of an adventure!

Up ahead, the track vanished into the forest, thick with trees. Tom's mouth went dry as Able Morris flicked the reins and dug his heels into Ferdy.

On they went, and on, then further still into the forest.

Tom kept looking from left to right. He peered into the darkness of the thick undergrowth. *Outlaws and robbers won't be interested in the likes of us*, he thought to himself. *They'll only be interested in rich people wearing expensive jewels or merchants with bags of gold coins.*

How wrong he was!

There was a noise up ahead. It sounded like a hoot of an owl, but even Tom knew enough about birds to know that owls didn't hoot in the daytime. It must be a signal!

It was. Moments later, Tom and Able were surrounded by a band of men dressed in brown.

The tallest man Tom had ever seen in his life was striding towards them. He was so tall that his head was higher off the ground than Able's, and Able was sitting on a horse!

"We have visitors!" laughed the man, his voice deep and booming. "Let's make them welcome, men."

Before Tom knew what was happening, he was dragged off the horse and stuffed into a sack.

****

The outlaws must have had sacks in all shapes and sizes, because they found one big enough for Able Morris.

He was a lot larger and struggled a lot more than Tom, so it took six outlaws to get him into his sack – and not before they had to stuff his hat into his mouth to stop him shouting, "Robbers! Outlaws! Murderers!" and a few other things far too rude to write down here.

Tom could hear all this going on, but couldn't see it because he was already in his sack, which had been tied shut at the top with rope.

It was quite comfy as outlaws' sacks went. The sacking it was made from wasn't too thick, so the evening light could still filter through it. It wasn't that itchy stuff either, which makes you want to scratch all the time.

Tom could have done with a cushion in his sack, but the ground where the sack had been dumped wasn't too lumpy. A window would have been nice too, but Tom didn't have too much to moan about – except, of course, for the fact that he'd been kidnapped by outlaws.

If he didn't manage to come up with an escape plan, he might never get to be a knight after all!

Tom grew tired of shouting, 'let me out!' In fact, he was just beginning to think that a short snooze might not be a bad idea, when he felt the sack being lifted and the rope round the top was untied. The next moment he was tipped onto the mossy ground.

Blinking, Tom looked around him. He was somewhere deep in the forest, sitting in the middle of a circle of outlaws, all armed with

stout, long sticks, bows and arrows. "Who are you?" Tom demanded. "And what have you done with Able Morris?"

The very tall man laughed. "At times like this, it is *we* who ask the questions," he boomed. The other men (for they were all men) burst out laughing.

"My name is Tom Dashwood," said Tom, pulling himself up to look tall, and dusting himself down. "My parents are Sir Simon and Lady Ann Dashwood."

"So Lord Dashwood of Dashwood Castle be your uncle?" said a rather jolly-looking outlaw. Like the others, he was dressed in brown.

"Yes he be – yes he *is*," said Tom with pride. "Now, I think you'd better let me and Able Morris go. My uncle will be sending out a whole army of knights to look for me."

"Oooh! I'm quaking in my boots," said the tall man, rudely.

"Well, you're not brave enough to tell me *your* names!" snapped Tom.

That wiped the smile off the man's face. "No-one tells me I'm not brave enough," said the man. "My name is Big Jim and we are the Green Men of Gressingham."

Tom looked at the men who surrounded him. Although they came in different shapes and sizes, they all wore the same sort of clothes.

"The *Green* Men of Gressingham?" asked Tom. Big Jim nodded. "Then why are you all dressed in *brown*?"

"Brown's cheaper than green and it hides the dirt better," said the jolly one. "We don't get much time to wash our clothes, being bold and brave outlaws. My name is Friendly."

18

Friendly held out his hand for Tom to shake. Shaking hands was to show that neither person was holding a weapon nor had one hidden up his sleeve.

Even though Friendly was an outlaw and a robber, Tom couldn't help liking him. He shook Friendly's hand. "I do think it would be better for all of us if you let me and Able Morris go," Tom said.

"You're a stubborn one," said Big Jim. "What are you doing in Gressingham Forest, Tom?"

"I'm on my way to the castle," said Tom. He saw no point in hiding the truth. "I'm going to learn to be a knight."

"The castle be a bad place," said Friendly.

"For outlaws, perhaps," said Tom, "but not for good, honest people!"

"And when were you last at the castle?" demanded another of the Green Men of Gressingham. The one called Fidget.

"I've never been there," Tom had to admit.

~~Fritz catcher~~

Fritz: great catcher

Nathan - Dancer   ← Check out

Maddie - Hose Crazy   dog videos

Allie - House Trasher

Deisel - Headstuck

Chapter 3
Robyn-in-the-Hat

"We can't blame the boy for his uncle's crimes if he's never even been to the castle," said Friendly, walking around Tom in a circle. "I say we let him go!"

Now Tom *really* liked him. I can't think why!

"And I say we hold him here and demand a ransom," said Big Jim. "Lord Dashwood will pay good money to get young Tom back alive."

Boo! Hiss! thought Tom.

"We could do with a few bags of gold!" cried another.

"That's it, then," said Big Jim. "We keep the boy and we set Able Morris free. He can go with a message to Lord Dashwood that young Tom is our prisoner."

"That's up to the boss, not us," said Friendly. The others fell silent.

All Tom could hear was Able Morris struggling in his sack, under a far-off tree. "I thought you were the boss," said Tom, looking up at Big Jim.

"Er, no," said Big Jim. "I'm only in charge until Robyn-in-the-Hat gets back."

"And Robyn is your leader?"

"Don't you know anything?" asked Friendly. "People sing songs about the great deeds of Robyn-in-the-Hat and the Green Men of Gressingham!"

"I don't get out much," Tom had to admit. "I've never been this far from home before – any new song takes ages to reach us."

"Well, you're a brave one, I'll say that for you," said a voice behind him.

Tom spun around just as a woman in a strange, brown hat came out from behind a bush.

"Some outlaws you are! Not one of you spotted me creeping up on you! I've been listening to every word you've been saying for the past ten minutes. What if I'd been a spy for Lord Dashwood?"

"But you're not. You're Robyn," grinned Friendly.

"So no harm be done!" said the other Green Men of Gressingham.

"So, you're Lord Dashwood's nephew," she said to Tom.

Robyn-in-the-Hat was dressed like all the outlaws, except for her hat. It was a very strange hat indeed, and Tom could see why it had become a part of her name. It was half hat and half mask. A brown, felt flap came down over the top part of her face. There were two holes, through which Tom could see a pair of sparkling, blue eyes.

He didn't think that he would recognise Robyn-in-the-Hat *without* her hat. "How come you wear a mask when none of your men do?" asked Tom.

"These men are what they appear to be, Tom," she said. "They're honest-to-goodness robbers and outlaws. It's the only life they lead. I, on the other hand, lead two lives, so that we can be," she paused to think of the right words, "more successful in what we do."

"I don't see why I should believe a word you say," said Tom. "When you told all those lies about my uncle –"

"Hold your tongue and keep quiet, boy," said Big Jim, with an angry look. "Outlaws we may be, but we aren't lying about Lord Dashwood."

"Cross my heart and hope to die, Tom," said Friendly. "Dashwood Castle and its lands may once have been a happy place, but not any more."

"Your uncle has brought in new taxes and sent out his Marshal, a man called Guppy, to collect them," said Robyn-in-the-Hat. "It's only fair that the peasants who work on your uncle's lands should pay him taxes, but in some cases, the peasants are being asked to give more than they own!"

Tom didn't know what to think. What would Robyn and the Green Men of Gressingham gain by lying to him?

"Dashwood Castle's dungeons are filled with prisoners, most of them good, honest people who've tried to stand up to your uncle," Robyn told Tom.

"But Able Morris said nothing of this to me," said Tom, and he pointed, nodding in the direction of the struggling sack.

"He's not likely to say anything if he's your uncle's man, is he, Master Tom?" said Robyn.

Suddenly there was another hooting signal. Big Jim clamped his huge hand across Tom's mouth. "Not a word," he whispered.

Fidget lifted a heavy, flat sword from a hiding place behind a rock and pressed the tip of it against Able Morris's sack. "If you don't stop struggling and groaning right now, I'll put an end to you," he hissed through clenched teeth.

Able Morris fell silent for the first time since he'd been taken prisoner.

Now every Green Man of Gressingham had a weapon in hand and was ready for action.

The last thing Robyn-in-the-Hat and her band of outlaws were expecting to see was a wounded man on a donkey.

"It's Max the Miller!" cried Friendly, and he rushed forward to help the man off his animal. While Friendly and Big Jim gently lifted the miller down and placed him on the ground, Fidget led the donkey to a bucket of water and let him drink.

"What happened, Max?" asked Robyn, dabbing his head with a piece of cloth – a *brown* piece of cloth.

"Lord Dashwood's men came demanding more taxes," groaned the miller. "When I said I had no more money left, they said they'd take Gee-Gee as payment instead." The miller let out an even bigger groan at the thought of it.

"You mean his horse?" gasped Tom. Horses were of great value to people in those days.

"No, his *daughter*," hissed Big Jim. "They have strange names in Max the Miller's family!"

Tom's jaw dropped.

"I tried to stop them. I tried," said Max.

"I'm sure you did your best," said Robyn. Tom could see through the holes in her mask that there were tears in her eyes.

"There were just too many of them," said the miller. "Too many."

"You must take some rest," said Robyn, patting the wounded man's arm.

"But what about Gee-Gee?" the miller protested. He tried to sit up but found the effort too painful, and lay down again.

"Don't you worry," said Robyn. "We'll get your Gee-Gee back, safe and well."

Max the Miller looked up at Big Jim, who looked down at him and nodded. "Robyn-in-the-Hat has given her word, Max," he said. "So it's as good as done."

Just then another Green Man of Gressingham arrived. Tom had not met this one. The man was dressed as a monk and was clutching a large, leather pouch.

"What kept you, Physic?" Robyn demanded. "Max needs the best medicines you have."

"And I need to see what I am doing," said Physic. "Bring me a light."

While Physic looked after Max the Miller, Robyn took Tom by the arm. "*Now* will you believe us?" she said.

"I-I suppose so," said Tom, though he still found it difficult to see his uncle as an evil man.

All his life he had heard such grand stories about his uncle and how one day Tom would become one of his knights.

Now that the time had come for Tom to begin his training as a knight – well, as a page and then a squire and then, *maybe*, a knight – he'd found out that his uncle was a feared and evil man!

"This must come as a big shock to you," said Robyn.

"It does," said Tom. "What are you going to do about rescuing the miller's daughter?"

"Gee-Gee? Well that depends on whether you are going to help us or not," said Robyn, from behind her mask.

"Me?" said Tom. "I thought I was the enemy. How can I help you?"

"The castle guards are expecting you and Able Morris to come back to the castle," Robyn explained. She began to stir the contents of a cooking pot, bubbling over an open fire. She was silent for a moment.

32

"If one," she paused and looked at the size of the sack with Able Morris in it, "or *two* of my Green Men can pretend to be Able Morris, and if you don't give us away –"

"Then I can try and free Gee-Gee once I'm inside!" cried Tom.

"Not just Gee-Gee," said Robyn. "You could let us in and we could attack Dashwood Castle and free everyone! We already have a plan to enter the castle, but going through the front gate with you would save a lot of time. You could give us the chance we've been waiting for!"

Tom felt a bit sick. "I'd like to help," he said. "I really would, but it seems wrong to betray my uncle by letting you into the castle. It's belonged to my family since it was built." He remembered his mother's parting words, *be brave and true.*

"I can understand how you feel," said Robyn, "but you saw what was done to poor old Max the Miller back there and he's just one of hundreds whose lives have been wrecked by your uncle's men."

"Can I give you my answer in the morning?" asked Tom. He suddenly felt very tired and very confused.

"Do you give me your word as Sir Simon's son that you won't try to escape?"

"I do," said Tom.

"Then you have until morning to decide whether to help us free Gee-Gee and the others," said Robyn.

Tom nodded.

Later that evening, after Tom had eaten supper, not as a prisoner but as a guest, the outlaws sang songs around the campfire.

It was a small fire so the light wouldn't be spotted by enemy spies. They sang very quietly so as not to be heard. In fact, instead of singing round the campfire, they were whispering round a damp fire!

Tom found it boring and soon drifted off to sleep. He awoke to find himself with someone's hand over his mouth. As his eyes became used to the darkness, Tom saw that the hand belonged to Able Morris.

"We must escape from this place," he whispered. "Come!"

Tom groaned. *What was he to do now?*

Chapter 4
To the Castle!

Tom looked at Able Morris, who seemed just the same even after all that time in the sack. "I can't," he whispered.

"Can't what?" asked Able Morris.

"Escape."

"Why?" asked Able Morris, with a worried frown. "Are you hurt? Have these villains wounded you in any way?"

Tom shook his head. "No," he hissed. "It's just that I've given Robyn-in-the-Hat my word that I won't try to escape."

"And I've promised your uncle, Lord Dashwood, that I will return safely with you to Dashwood Castle," said Able Morris.

"Oh dear," said Tom, "that leaves us in rather a mess then, doesn't it?"

Able nodded towards the edge of the camp and began tiptoeing off.

Tom knew he must follow. When they were far enough away not to be heard by the sleeping outlaws, they went on talking in hushed voices.

"Let me think," said Able.

Tom studied Able's face in the early morning light. If only he knew who to trust. Robyn-in-the-Hat, or Able Morris? Was Able really hiding the truth from him? Was his uncle really an evil man?

"I have it, Master Tom!" whispered Able Morris. "I know how you can leave this place without breaking your promise!"

"How?" whispered Tom, wide awake now.

"As my prisoner!" grinned Able and, for the second time in 24 hours, Tom found himself in a sack! This time with a gag in his mouth so he couldn't cry out.

Able Morris must have been able to steal back his own horse. Tom saw it was Ferdy the minute he was let out of the bag, many hours later. Tom lay sprawled on the ground staring up at Ferdy's head and the blue sky above. "I'm not sure if I should be thanking you or shouting at you!" said Tom to Able Morris, blinking in the bright light of mid-morning.

"This way, you don't break your promise," said Able Morris. He'd just tipped Tom out of the sack and was folding it up neatly. "You didn't break any promises. I took you away from the camp against your will."

"But *they* don't know that," Tom protested. He got to his feet. "Where are we?"

"Look behind you," said Able.

Tom turned and there, in all its glory, was Dashwood Castle. He gasped. It was even grander than he'd imagined. It had high walls of thick stone, with a round tower at each corner. There was a moat of black water around it, and there were soldiers keeping watch. Their polished helmets glinted in the morning sun.

Tom's father had described the castle to him a thousand times, but nothing had prepared Tom for how he'd feel as he stood

looking at this truly splendid building. This was Dashwood Castle, and *he* was a Dashwood!

In that moment, he felt so proud. Then he remembered everything Robyn-in-the-Hat had said. He thought of Max the Miller. He would ask his uncle about these things as soon as possible. Tom was very excited. "Can we go inside?" he asked.

"That's why we're here," grinned Able Morris. He climbed up onto Ferdy and, once again, pulled Tom up after him. They rode over a bridge that led to a small watchtower, called a barbican, where they were met by a guard.

"Halt! Who goes there?" the guard demanded, waving his pike staff at them.

"Able Morris and Master Tom Dashwood," said Able. His face broke into a grin. "Let us through will you, there's a good chap."

The guard did not return the smile. "You may enter," he said, raising his hand as a signal to the guards at the main gate of the castle.

There was a grating noise and the drawbridge was lowered between the barbican and the castle. They rode across it through the gateway and into the courtyard. Able Morris and Tom had arrived at last.

No sooner had Tom slid off Ferdy than a tall, thin, red-haired man in a dark-blue cloak appeared through an archway. "What took you so long?" he demanded.

"We were kidnapped by outlaws, Marshal," said Able Morris, holding his squishy hat in his hands. He sounded nervous. "But we escaped."

The Marshal stared at Able Morris. "If you say so," he said. "Bring the boy to his uncle.

Lord Dashwood wants to see him and we do so like to keep his lordship happy, don't we?"

"Y-Yes, Sire," nodded Able Morris.

Ferdy, meanwhile, was being led across the courtyard to the stable block by one of the many servants rushing here and there inside the castle walls.

Tom could hear the drawbridge being raised behind them. It shut with a final clang.

"Are you Marshal Guppy?" Tom asked the man in the dark-blue cloak. Tom had expected him to be bigger and meaner, from the way the outlaws had been talking about him.

"I am," said Marshal Guppy, staring deep into his eyes. "You have heard of me?"

"Yes, Sire," said Tom, suddenly feeling very small and lost in this huge castle packed with people.

"You've heard good things, I hope?" said Marshal Guppy, turning his head away. He laughed a nasty laugh. "I'm glad you seem none the worse for your harsh treatment by the outlaws. Now, go to your uncle!"

****

45

Lord Dashwood couldn't have been more different from Marshal Guppy if he'd tried. He was a big, round, cheerful man with a huge moustache. There was an odd chuckle in every sentence he spoke.

He was sitting on a huge chair with his left leg propped up on a wooden stool. It was bound up in bandages.

"Come, let me take a look at you, Tom!" he said when Able Morris brought him into the room. "My! My brother Simon's baby has grown into a fine lad!" He beckoned Tom over and gave him a slap on the back and a hug. "Welcome to Dashwood Castle!"

"Hello, Uncle," said Tom. "We were taken prisoner by the Green Men of Gressingham!" His words were spilling out. "They said that –"

At that very moment, Marshal Guppy came striding into the room. "Time for your morning medicine, your lordship," he said and bowed very, *very* low. He handed Tom's uncle a silver goblet of hot liquid, which Lord Dashwood drank in one gulp.

"Thank you, Guppy," he chuckled. "I don't know what I'd do without you. You're my nursemaid, my advisor, my Marsh ... Marsh ... Marsh-sh-sh ..." With that, his eyelids fluttered, drooped and well and truly closed.

"You must leave his lordship to sleep now," said the Marshal. "He's not a well man. Able Morris, show the lad to his room." With that, he picked up the empty goblet and left the room.

"My uncle's not well? Why didn't you tell me this, Able?" Tom demanded.

"Orders," said Able Morris. "Lord Dashwood doesn't want people to think he's weak.

They want him to protect them and decide what needs to be done. He is in charge of the lives of all the peasants for miles around."

"What's wrong with him?" asked Tom.

"He hurt his foot when he was out hunting. Since then, he has never been strong and spends his days here in his room. The medicine often makes him drowsy. Sometimes he sleeps right through the day. I spend my time here with him. That's why he needs Marshal Guppy to take charge of things for him."

"And does Marshal Guppy do what my uncle wants?" Tom muttered.

"What do you mean?" demanded Able, opening a chest and removing a large blanket which he tucked round his sleeping master.

"Well, it sounds like Guppy gets a free hand to do what he likes, in my uncle's name – if the people don't like it, they blame my uncle!"

"But that can't be true!" Able Morris protested. "I mean, I would know if there were strange things going on, wouldn't I?"

"How would *you* know? Don't you spend all your time in here with my uncle? You've no idea what's going on out in the villages or down in the dungeons."

"Well, er – why would the Marshal have risked sending me off to bring you here, if I might see or hear something that I shouldn't? He could have sent one of the guards."

Able Morris opened a wooden shutter and sunlight streamed through a glassless window into Lord Dashwood's room.

"Was it Marshal Guppy or my uncle who asked you to fetch me here?" asked Tom, peering out of the window. It was a long drop down to the moat below and he felt a bit sick.

"Your uncle –"

"And Marshal Guppy wants my uncle to think that everything he wants done, *is* done. So he can't openly go against his wishes. That's why *you* had to be the one to go and fetch me," Tom argued.

Able Morris sat in a chair by his master who was now snoring. "I don't know what to think," sighed Able.

"If only I could get to the dungeons to see if Max the Miller's daughter, Gee-Gee, is being held a prisoner there."

There was a scuttling sound, and Tom caught sight of a shadow moving in the corridor. "Someone was listening at the doorway!" he cried. "They'll probably report back to Marshal Guppy and then we're done for!"

They ran to the doorway. "Then we must act quickly," said Able. "Let's look in the dungeons and, if you're right, we'll tell your uncle everything when he wakes up – follow me."

Chapter 5
Time for Action

Able may have been a little on the large side – in fact, he was a *lot* on the large side – but Tom had trouble keeping up with him as he dashed through a maze of corridors and down the stone stairs.

Tom knew that he'd never be able to find his way back on his own. They were going deeper and deeper into the castle.

"What if they won't let us in?" Tom panted.

"Then you must try to find a way to have a peek inside whilst I distract the guard," said Able.

At last, they reached the dungeon. "Lord Dashwood has asked me to inspect this place," Able told a rather dopey-looking guard with stubble on his chin.

"Let me see your orders," said the guard.

"I don't have any written orders," said Able, trying to sound as proud and indignant as he could. "I am Able Morris, his lordship's personal assistant, not a common soldier who needs written orders."

"Well," said the guard, "I *am* a common soldier and I *do* need written orders, Sire. I'm not going to risk my neck by letting you past without –"

While the two men were talking, Tom slipped behind the guard's back and, keeping to the shadows, made his way down the corridor.

At the end, was a thick door instead of a stone wall. Level with Tom's ankles were two windows each with a grating on either side of the door.

Through the grating, Tom could see down to a gloomy room below, with straw on the floor. It was full of prisoners. Hundreds of them. Some chained. Some free to move about. Men, women and children. Young and old.

The one thing they all had in common was that they looked thin and dirty.

Tom's heart sank. They all looked so sad. He pressed his face up against the grating. "Pssssssssssst! Pssssssssssssst!"

"Who is it?" called one of the prisoners.

"Ssssh! Keep your voice down!" whispered Tom in a panic. "Is Gee-Gee the miller's daughter there?"

There was some movement and, after a while, a small, blonde girl with tears running down her cheeks was lifted up to the grating. She clutched the bars and peered through them at Tom. "What is it?" she whispered. "Is my father all right? Who are you?"

"I'm a friend," whispered Tom. "Your father is fine. He was wounded but Physic, one of the Green Men of Gressingham, is looking after him. The Green Men are making plans to rescue you all. Be brave. Tell the others that help *will* come. Robyn-in-the-Hat is on her way."

The poor girl shouted with excitement. The conversation at the end of the corridor stopped at once, and Tom heard the guard running in his direction. There was nowhere to hide.

Instead of trying to dodge him, Tom dashed straight at him and then, at the very last moment, dived between his legs. This sent the guard toppling to the stone floor with a nasty crunch as Tom and Able ran away.

"Ooooooooh! My nose is bleeding!" the guard wailed as Tom followed Able down the endless passages.

At last, Able led Tom into a room with a large, built-in, oak wardrobe along one wall. In fact, the whole room was called The Wardrobe, because this was where the robes were warded (looked after).

Able checked to see if they were alone. They seemed to be. "Well?" he asked.

"Gee-Gee the miller's daughter and hundreds of other prisoners were there," said Tom. "I believe everything Robyn-in-the-Hat said. I know it's difficult for you to believe, because you and my uncle have been tricked, but I think Dashwood Castle has turned evil. It's the outlaws who are on the side of good!"

"If you're right, Master Tom, then the guard outside your uncle's room who heard us making plans will have told Marshal Guppy. The dungeon guard will also report us and by then, it'll be too late to do anything," said a worried Able. "Marshal Guppy will lock us up too. He'll make up some story as to why we aren't around and your uncle is used to trusting him."

"It shouldn't be too hard to trick your old fool of an uncle. He spends much of his life asleep, drugged by one of my potions," sneered Marshal Guppy as he stepped out of the oak wardrobe. It led to one of the many secret passages in the castle. "I think I'll arrange a little swordfight. Poor Tom is keen to have a go and silly old Able Morris is keen to let him have one. I can see there will be a lot of blood and broken bones. Take them away."

Two soldiers stepped out of the passage and grabbed Able and Tom, pressing the tips of their swords into their backs.

Chapter 6
Uninvited Guests

We often forget about one of the most important things they had to remember when they built a medieval castle.

We all think about the drawbridge, the moat, the thick doors, the high walls and the tall towers with their thin arrow slits. The brainier amongst us may even consider where the castle was built, on high ground for example, to make it easier to defend.

But what we often forget is the well – the water supply. Without water, you die of thirst!

Dashwood Castle had a large well in its own room on the ground floor. The water was fairly clean by medieval standards, but you'd still be glad to drink beer instead. Even first thing in the morning.

That Sunday morning, however, something very strange was going on in the well room. Every few minutes a head would appear at the top of the well and a naked man would climb out. Each man carried a weapon and a waterproof sack. Out of the sack, he pulled a dry, brown monk's robe which he slipped on. He then tucked his weapon inside and pulled the hood up over his head.

The men were all different shapes and sizes. One was huge. One was round and the others were everything in between. Soon the room was packed with hooded monks, though it's unlikely that they had come to pray in the chapel. When all who were going to clamber out of the well had clambered out, the monks drifted into the castle courtyard.

The first Tom knew about the arrival of the monks was when a friendly face appeared at the high window of his prison cell.

The friendly face did indeed belong to Friendly, the jolliest of the Green Men of Gressingham. "Fear not, Tom, help is at hand!" he whispered.

"I thought you thought I was the enemy!" cried Tom.

"Never!" smiled Friendly. "You told the other prisoners that help was on the way. You're a prisoner in your uncle's own castle.

That makes you a friend, Master Tom." He threw one end of a thick rope down to him.

Tom climbed up the rope and squeezed through the bars of his prison before you could say, 'Down with Marshal Guppy!' "What about the others?" he asked.

"Big Jim has freed the prisoners from the main dungeon, and your friend Able was among them," said Friendly. He made the rope into a neat coil and hid it inside his monk's robe. They were in some empty inner, inner part of the castle. "If they catch us, they'll only out-number us by 500 to 1, so we should be fine. We fight best when the odds are against us."

"But if we can get to my uncle and tell him what's been going on, then we may be able to turn the odds in our favour and win," said Tom.

Friendly frowned. "I don't know if us Green Men have ever taken on a mission when the odds were on our side. That *would* be something new!"

"If only I knew my way around the castle," Tom groaned. "I haven't the foggiest idea how to find my uncle's room."

"Have no fear!" said Friendly. "I have a map." He put his hand up one sleeve. Nothing. "Somewhere ..." he said, pulling a rolled up map out of the other. "Now, let's see."

Chapter 7
Attack!

Tom's uncle was very surprised to be woken up by his nephew and a jolly-looking monk. "Good morning, young Tom. What's going on?"

"You've been tricked, Uncle!" Tom told him. "Ever since you hurt your foot and couldn't get around your castle and lands, Marshal Guppy has been doing terrible things in your name. He's been over-taxing the peasants, and I'll bet he's been slipping the money into his own pocket. He's also been putting good, honest people in prison – men, women and children too. I saw them with my own eyes last night."

Lord Dashwood looked at Friendly in horror. "Is this true?" he asked, as he struggled to sit up.

"It is, my lord," said Friendly, "though sadly, I thought these wrong-doings were on *your* orders until Tom told me what was really going on."

"I must do something to put things right!" gasped Lord Dashwood. "Where is Able Morris? Is he one of Marshal Guppy's men, or is he still loyal to me?"

"He's *most* loyal, Uncle," said Tom.

"You don't know how happy I am to hear that," said Lord Dashwood.

"But Able Morris was taken prisoner," Tom went on. He told his uncle everything that had happened since Able had come to fetch him from the Manor House and what they had discovered since then.

As Tom talked, he and Friendly helped to dress his lordship in his finest armour (which wasn't easy because he was hopping around on one leg).

"So the Green Men are here right now, setting the prisoners free," said Lord Dashwood. "This is the perfect time to strike back. Tom Dashwood, you will be my walking stick. I will lean on you. No more talk. Now – to action!"

Many of the guards and servants soon saw his lordship up and about, with Tom and a jolly monk beside him. They were surprised to see their master walking round but they were pleased too. They bowed as he made his way to the courtyard.

In the courtyard itself, they were greeted by an amazing sight. A group of monks and freed prisoners, many of them in rags, were in arm-to-arm combat with the castle guards.

The monks had thrown back their hoods and it was easy to see that they were the Green Men of Gressingham. They all seemed to be enjoying a good punch-up. Fists, arrows and rocks were flying everywhere.

As Tom arrived on the scene, Big Jim was picking up a soldier in each hand and banging their heads together with a pleasing 'THUNK'. The attack from within was so unexpected that everything seemed to be going the outlaws' way.

Then the tide suddenly turned.

Marshal Guppy clattered into the courtyard with a group of heavily armed knights.

"Kill them all!" cried Marshal Guppy, drawing his sword, and the knights drew their swords too.

"WAIT!" boomed the loud voice of someone who was used to being in command.

The knights hesitated. It was a voice they knew well but had not heard for some time. It belonged to their lord and master, Lord Dashwood.

Helped by Tom, he limped forward, and stood there, head and shoulders above the crowd, on the stone steps of the chapel. "STOP FIGHTING!" he shouted.

The effect was amazing. Even the outlaws and freed prisoners stopped to see what was happening.

"There will be no killing here today!" Lord Dashwood told them. "Though someone may soon hang for the bad deeds done in my name."

"The old fool doesn't know what he is saying," cried Marshal Guppy. "Why do you think I've been put in charge? He's lost his mind!"

"*I* am your master, not Marshal Guppy!" Lord Dashwood reminded them. He looked every inch a lord and ruler as he stood on the chapel steps in his gleaming armour.

Tom stood proudly at his side.

Marshal Guppy had made a bad mistake. Being a knight was based on being loyal to one's lord. You did what he said even if you didn't always like what he asked of you. Many of the knights had been unhappy at the orders Marshal Guppy had given them but, because they thought they were from Lord Dashwood, they had carried them out. Now it was clear that Marshal Guppy had been acting on his *own*.

Marshal Guppy could see that his run of good luck was over. "Come, Sir Clarence!" he said to the one evil knight who'd been in on his nasty plan from the start. "It's time to move on!" He dug his spurs into his horse's side and galloped towards the gatehouse. "Lower the drawbridge!" he yelled.

The guards in the gatehouse had no idea what had been going on in the castle. They followed the Marshal's orders. "He's going to get away!" cried Tom.

"Don't be so sure of that, Master Tom!" laughed Big Jim, lifting up a couple of soldiers from the cobbled floor and dusting them down. "No hard feelings, ay?" he said to them.

Everyone rushed to the drawbridge in time to see Marshal Guppy and Sir Clarence gallop halfway across – only to find their way was blocked by a lone figure on foot.

It was Robyn-in-the-Hat herself!

"ROBYN! ROBYN!" cheered the Green Men.

With a brief nod to the crowd and a clever twist of her staff she knocked Marshal Guppy from his horse. He flew off in a graceful curve, fell into the inky moat and sank like a sack of stones.

The second SPLASH could hardly be heard, because the crowd was cheering so loudly. Sir Clarence had joined his evil

master, Marshal Guppy, in the moat. A moment later, he bobbed up to the surface, spluttering and choking in the foul water.

"Where's Guppy?" asked Tom, running onto the drawbridge and looking into the moat. "Is he escaping underwater?"

Robyn-in-the-Hat dived into the moat and vanished for some time. Everyone waited in agony until she came up again. Her sodden felt mask was clinging flat against her face. She was holding Marshal Guppy. A dozen pairs of arms pulled them to safety.

"He weighs a ton!" Robyn gasped. When she tried to lift his cloak, she soon discovered why.

Coins tumbled out of the wet cloak onto the wood of the drawbridge. "He has gold stitched into his lining!" Robyn laughed.

The secret treasure which he had hidden away in case he ever had to flee the castle had nearly killed him!

Helped by Friendly, Lord Dashwood walked onto the bridge. Just then, Able Morris ran out from among the freed prisoners, and stood at his master's side.

"Hello, my loyal friend," said his lordship, with a beaming smile. "Glad to see you're safe and sound." Then he turned to Robyn. "I have much to thank you for," he said.

"But I'd like to say how sorry we are," said Robyn-in-the-Hat. "If it wasn't for your nephew Tom, we'd still think that you had given the orders for all this cruelty and wrong-doing. We should have known that you are a good man."

****

The next night there was much feasting in the castle, with all of Lord Dashwood's friends from miles around invited to a banquet. Even Tom's parents were there. His mother was crying (for joy this time).

People who hadn't seen his lordship for months, and who had heard how ill and frail he was, were delighted to find him fit and well. Physic had taken a look at his bad leg and nearly cured it already.

Guests of honour were the Green Men of Gressingham. But their leader, Robyn, was nowhere to be seen.

"Who are you looking for?" asked a voice.

Tom turned in his seat to see a beautiful young woman in a long, green dress of the finest silk. She sat down next to him at the table. "I'm looking for Robyn-in-the-Hat, m'lady," he told her.

"You have met the leader of the outlaws?" she asked. "She sounds most exciting."

"She is," said Tom. "Her Green Men kidnapped me, but we soon became friends."

"Is she beautiful?" asked the lady, with a strange smile on her lips.

"I've never seen her face," Tom had to admit. He looked at the lady beside him. She had a pair of sparkling, blue eyes.

Tom's uncle banged a golden goblet on the table. "A toast!" he cried, jumping to his feet.

Everyone in the great hall of Dashwood Castle stood up. "To the Green Men of Gressingham."

They all raised their goblets. "The Green Men of Gressingham!" they cried.

The lady with the sparkling blue eyes winked at Tom.

Could she be? No, surely not – but then again, she might be.

Who is Barrington Stoke?

Barrington Stoke was a famous and much-loved story-teller. He travelled from village to village carrying a lantern to light his way. He arrived as it grew dark and when the young boys and girls of the village saw the glow of his lantern, they hurried to the central meeting place. They were full of excitement and expectation, for his stories were always wonderful.

Then Barrington Stoke set down his lantern. In the flickering light the listeners were enthralled by his tales of adventure, horror and mystery. He knew exactly what they liked best and he loved telling a good story. And another. And then another. When the lantern burned low and dawn was nearly breaking, he slipped away. He was gone by morning, only to appear the next day in some other village to tell the next story.

Barrington Stoke would like to thank all its readers for commenting on the manuscript before publication and in particular:

Lindsay Allen
Olivia Aylott
Ben Clifford
Zak Degerland
Sophie Ferguson
Nicholas Freeston
Emma Hotchkiss
Matthew Hulf
Declan Illing
Edward Jennings
Jacob Jolleys
Gavin Jones
Kieron Kelly

Alex King
Lesley Leeding
Jonathan Riordan
Ted Sarder
Gavin Smyth
Melissa Taylor
Scott Thwaites
Jonatha Trotter
Sarah Warr
Louise Jane Wellings
Mrs A. Wellings
Kane L. White
Sam Wilkinson

Become a Consultant!

Would you like to give us feedback on our titles before they are published? Contact us at the address or website below – we'd love to hear from you!

Barrington Stoke, 10 Belford Terrace, Edinburgh EH4 3DQ
Tel: 0131 315 4933 Fax: 0131 315 4934
E-mail: info@barringtonstoke.co.uk
Website: www.barringtonstoke.co.uk

If you loved this story, why don't you read...

Living with Vampires

by Jeremy Strong

Are your parents normal? Kevin's parents are really odd. They can turn people into zombies. Blood is their favourite drink. Even worse, they are coming to the school disco! How can Kevin get his parents to behave normally so he can impress the beautiful Miranda?

You can order this book directly from:
Macmillan Distribution Ltd, Brunel Road, Houndmills,
Basingstoke, Hampshire RG21 6XS
Tel: 01256 302699